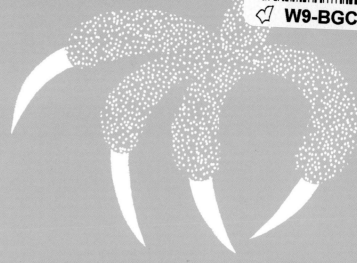

my BEST friend

Rob Hodgson

Frances Lincoln
Children's Books

Hi there!

I'm Mouse and I want to tell you
about my best friend . . .

Giant Owl!

We've been buddies ever since Giant Owl
brought me to live at the tree.

I'm so lucky Giant Owl found me.
I think we were destined to be best friends.

After all, we have so much fun!

We play chase together . . .

and sometimes Giant Owl nearly catches me . . .

but not quite.

Giant Owl's favorite game is hide and seek.

I'm so good at hiding. I can play for hours!

When we stop playing, Giant Owl always shares the tastiest snacks with me.

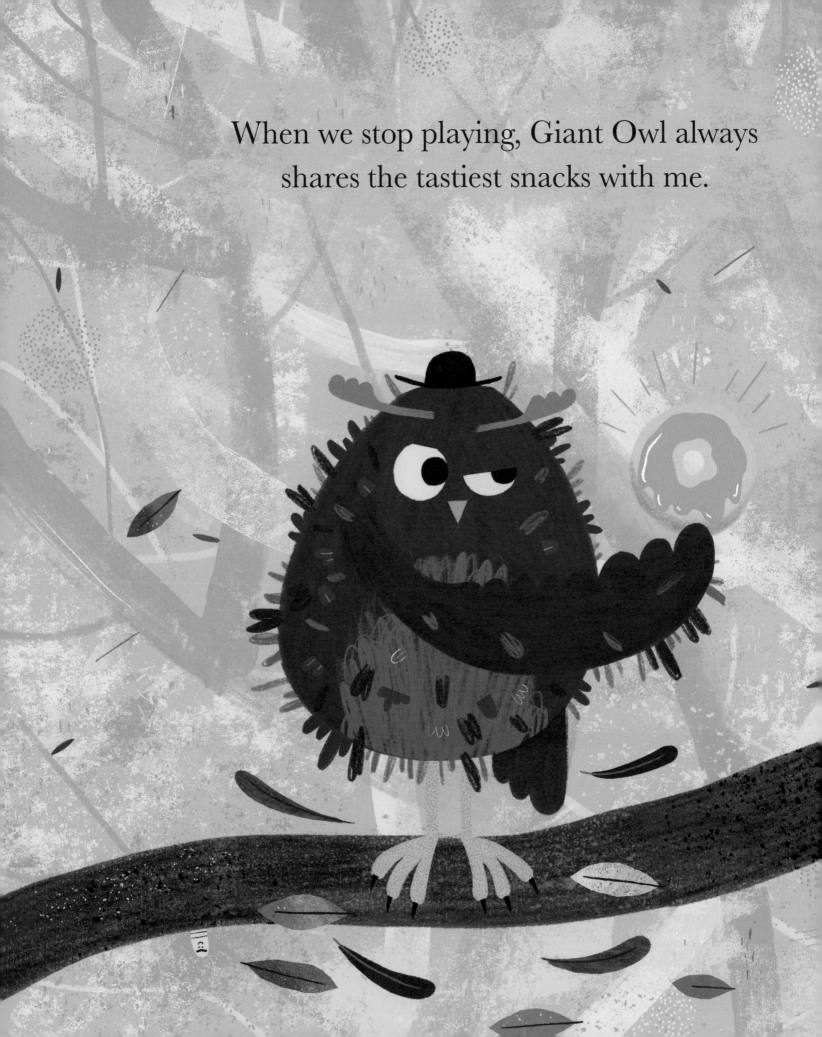

I'm so lucky to have such a generous best friend.

I love donuts, and Giant Owl
always gives me more . . .

and more . . .

and I eat them all up.

Every last one.

Occasionally I do have my doubts about our friendship.

Like, sometimes when I want to go for a walk,

or just be by myself for a while,

Giant Owl is *always* there. Having a best friend
can be annoying sometimes.

But I know it's just because Giant Owl loves me so much.

That's why Giant Owl always remembers my birthday and gives me great presents.

My own house?!

I'm so lucky to have such a thoughtful best friend.

My favorite thing of all about having a
best friend is sleepovers.

In fact, we had a sleepover just last night.
But when I woke up . . .

I found myself here with the lights turned out.

Where am I?

If only Giant Owl was here to
help me figure out this mess.

Gurrrgle.

Blurrrble.

Oooh.

Eeeeeeeeeeeee…

BUUUUURRRRRRRP!

Giant Owl!

You saved me.

You're my best friend in the whole world!

For Alba—R.H.

Inspiring | Educating | Creating | Entertaining

Brimming with creative inspiration, how-to projects, and useful information to enrich your everyday life, Quarto Knows is a favourite destination for those pursuing their interests and passions. Visit our site and dig deeper with our books into your area of interest: Quarto Creates, Quarto Cooks, Quarto Homes, Quarto Lives, Quarto Drives, Quarto Explores, Quarto Gifts, or Quarto Kids.

The illustrations were created using mixed and digital media

Set in Baskerville

Published and edited by Katie Cotton
Designed by Andrew Watson
Production by Caragh McAleenan

Manufactured in Guangdong, China TT022020

1 3 5 7 9 8 6 4 2